Copyright © 2023 Glenbard South High School
All rights reserved.

Sonder *n.*
The realization that each random passerby is living a life as vivid and complex as your own—populated with their own ambitions, friends, routines, worries and inherited craziness—an epic story that continues invisibly around you like an anthill sprawling deep underground, with elaborate passageways to thousands of other lives that you'll never know exist, in which you might appear only once, as an extra sipping coffee in the background, as a blur of traffic passing on the highway, as a lighted window at dusk.

-The Dictionary of Obscure Sorrows

Dedication

Once in their teenage years, a human being doesn't really grow *up* so much as they grow *out*. They learn to take up their share of space. They learn what their presence means in the world and to others. They learn to broaden their social sphere and to recognize that letting others in is the epitome of the human endeavor. If they are truly thoughtful, and willing to see beyond themselves, then they learn to recognize that each individual has a story. Each person they interact with has a voice and thoughts and an identity that is just as important and valid as their own. By opening this book, you embark on that experience…to be let into the minds and lives of dozens of individuals who have put themselves on the page. We ask that, as you read, you embrace that sense of sonder and take it with you into the trappings of your life. Into traffic when someone cuts you off. Into the subway car with the loud phone talker. Into the elevator and the grocery store and the waiting room. We ask that you do your level best to see, as these students are learning to see, that each person has a story to tell and that each story adds to the beauty of this world.

Poetry.

SIT WITH ME
BY DANIEL BARATKA

Sit with me, Says the man looking distant, so far away
He must have felt my stare for I made no noise
He pats the spot next to him, and slowly I follow his
old hollow hand

I know why you're here he states

His gaze still doesn't stray
I repeat his statement, now my question
And he laughs at this in a curious way

He smiles and nods as agreement escapes his lips
His hands are calm and feet are quiet
No sign of disappointment, not one simple display

Tracing his jawline I stare in wonder

His lips cracked but gentle in the cool autumn's day
Yet he seems warm and soothed in a strange but simple
manner
His postures relaxed and shoulders straight
He's known this day approached

He speaks again now in a mumble
Not straight in a common way
His words twist and bend
As letters dance off his tongue

Finally he's sung his prayer
and looks up as if finally done

Strange, this human is

Sitting lonely on this bench
He ponders silently
as if death does not sit with him
The questions he could ask
But he's silent, he's ready

My posture stiffens and my legs creak
I stand tall like the trees and tower the old man
With a cold dead hand
I stretch out towards him

He looks up with a smile, tears
Not of fear or sadness
Of acceptance
Gratitude

Up with a groan as his hand greets mine
With a long breath then a sigh
He asks only one question

Is it painful?
And finally a glimpse of fear breaks through
A smile creeps into my teeth
And this old rib cage chuckles

No, not at all I say
And then we are away

DAY 28: BIOLOGICAL FATE   BY HANS HERRERA

There's a corner in the science wing diverting two paths
Windows to a highway, another leads to class

In AP Bio we're mumbling hereditary while reading on rats
But at this crossroads, I dawdle, a Schrödinger's cat

I had heard the emergency exit say:
"To be closed in school hours, all during the day."

To be used in a fire, during time of crisis
To be stared at by students left with their own devices

But on the other side, just a walk through cut
dead grass to Butterfield
Where stimuli stutters but cars don't yield.

Grey skies leave views dull and cold
Where plastered roadkill doesn't make it to "old."

In sixth period, we're piping blood and spit
Sweat and tears from this great red pit

They're whispering stories, swabbing gossip
Festering amusement fresh off of the hot lip

Up on the lawn, exhaustive wind blows
It tangles the whisker, it scratches the nose

The asphalt's sky-pale on tired stone
Heart echoes a scream, mouth mutters a groan

This RNA, DNA, a molecule light
Binds me to myself by force stronger than sight

Maybe I ought to turn to ol' Joshua for help
Hand on Bible, pastor preaches with: "Welp,

There's not much prayer we can do
For someone quite as lascivious as you."

So I'm shoved like a stray onto the street,
All rugged-burned and effigied

Like a mangled faux cotton pet
In sleep recession or narco-fret

Chip on my shoulder, trip onto the road
Just impulse of nerve, hormone from the node.

They wouldn't miss me by the time we reach Lit
While they're reading mythology, a truck's got me hit.

Maybe in eighth, Doyle's reading some Aeschylus
How a curséd boy managed to still get the best of us.

Do you think Orestes could best these long-fated lies?
With his parents wearing masks with dark-sullen eyes

Do you think Orestes could do better than rest?
When his mother uses family to put word-ax to test

Do you think Orestes could have changed his life?
Escaped furies that wrought such genealogical strife

Orestes was man, less lives than cat
Divine violence devoured him, and that was that.

So where am I now, in hypothetical split
Less glory than legend, more missing than myth

There's paths not travelled, there's Robert Frost
Either way I'll end up tomb with name embossed

The world it's turning and it won't stop
Even if self-born force makes me drop

But if that's the secret, should I go on and fight
Should cells keep renewing, in tumor or blight?

Why do bodies keep fighting to very end?
When stage four takes them, does it offend?

Hallways are peripatetic in this purgation
Emotional catharsis or intellect clarification

Is it strength to fight against fate
Or cowardice to sit and wait

Or is it the other way around
That at times accepting can be something profound

Anagnorisis, apex predator, man on top
Still deals to fate, still gambles the lot

What happened to Orestes, I can't tell
Was he forgiven or descended to hell

Story's not finished, turning the page
Maybe furies can be kindly, pacify their rage

And perhaps my children will write of me in rhyme
How I spoke out-of-tune or at the wrong time

And even my peers toil to overcome
With parables to sing, hosannas to hum

A drum of heartbeat, a life force threading loom
Will have troubles to taste, loves to bloom

So if we are just cells and that is all
Is that a justified reason to crawl into a ball?
Just take a step, find a sip in your dried up well
Some things may be written, some things aren't spelled.

Just breathe.
Float. Fall. Grieve.

Everything in your life has led to this chance
Take back your adrenaline, your lysine, your tryptophans.

Everything in your life has led to this moment,
From day waking dreams or nightmares so potent

Everything in your life has led you to here
So much to learn yet so much to fear.

Everything in your life has led you to this
Not even night-slitted eyes can see into abyss

Life is for living, even with debt
Curiosity kills cats but you're not dead yet

Somewhere there is sonder, sundering someone else
In here can be wonder, infinitely multiplying by itself.

Feeling wrong is part of the way you know,
Black and white isn't the same as letting go.

It's awkward, it's stupid, it feels dumb
Flowing in and out of what's to come.

Biology and Butterfield, Cat and Mouse
Bloodlines are fluid, even in the great Greek House.

Jessica Nakayama / Yugen Wave

"
In conversation with Richard Hoggart, [Tony Harrison] explains that without the rhythmical formality of poetry he would be less able to confront, without losing hope, his favored themes of death, time and social injustice. "That rhythmical thing is like a life-support system. It means I feel I can go closer to the fire, deeper into the darkness . . . I know I have this rhythm to carry me to the other side". "

SHE'S WEAVING WONDER   BY HANS HERRERA

Sara's siesta waiting at home
Had been anticipated in her every bone
She rattled like the yellow bus
Or knots up hair she'd constantly fuss

At the end of her day, she'd untie her shoes
Sling off her backpack, put stress on snooze.
"Homework can wait," she'd presume
When all she needed was her rainbow loom

With her tools, she saw how the world could be
And wielding her hands, she'd weave a tapestry
Like those folktales she'd defy the odds,
And make bracelets better than those
"Paper Instruction Gods!"

With each band she chose, she mended a seam
And took a vibrant step into history's screen
Like those wondrous, looming trailblazers of old
That all the grown-ups had highlighted with BOLD.

A red ring, like Ruby Bridges' dress
As her stride helped put division to rest
Only six years old, with a stature so small
She lead a path forward, an education for all

Could she have done the same? Sara couldn't say,
But Ruby got what her parents fought for everyday
How they took so much pressure for their own little jewel
Held high against pickett, backlash, and spool

An orange band reminded her of Mae Jemison's place
The first black woman to ever travel to space
Her tangerine suit floating among the stars
Becoming a pin-prick of light in the pit of tar

She remembered her mama put Mae on TV,
Trekking with the next generation as she ought to be
Maybe one day Sara could pave her career
And like Mae, explore that final frontier

A golden ring, like Miss Angelou's mines
How she channeled her voice in the most troubled of times
Wrote psalms for her sorrows, freed her fight
How even when silent she still had her sight

To reclaim the world despite what it brings
To understand why the caged bird sings
To wipe back her tears in the struggle of cries
And like the sun at daybreak, still she'd rise.

With another loop, she's pulled to Madame C.J's greens
How Miss Walker's been working since her early teens
Perfecting a tin of her own "Wonderful Hair Grower"
Inadvertently, also becoming a sower

Of dreams for black women across the states
Who could provide for their families,
put food on their plates
Her beam of wealth and agency
Styling her hair up with dignity

Sara's hands keep moving as she conjures someone new,
Who wore her scrubs sky-brilliant blue
Alexa Canady, her mama knew
Was out saving lives like rent was DUE

Neurosurgeon and miracle-maker
Finding joy in making kids feel a "little bit safer"
She powered pediatrics with her wit
And used soul like medicine as an advocate

With another ring, Sara was brought to recall
A poster of Grace Jones her mama hung up on the wall
Her modeled majesty in indigo-tint
Who's radiance was clear even in squint

A luxurious icon that needs no pearls
To spread her voice through the fashion world
She'd strut the runway, hit her mark
A beacon from Stonewall to Central Park

The Color Purple, her mama'd say
Spread a message she'd need every day
Alice's words for times of crisis
Is to be thankful for her own devices

To remain present, to simply be
No matter the struggles that wrought Celie
To wrap herself in her lavender love
To be thankful for standing by the Lord God above

Sara's design with every chance,
Brought color and light in its dexterital dance
She held it out before herself
Knowing she's created something with invaluable wealth

A rainbow made of every hand
Stretched from here back to the African land
Where every man or woman to be
Could have traced their roots of ancestry

Curved and arched like history's spine
A back-bone brought by Black work divine
With hand climbing out of the sea
Reaching towards epiphany

That wraps the rainbow 'round her wrist
So she may lead with love, not iron fist
Bracelet made of simply rubber
Gave her hope she'd one day be on front-page cover

She'd remember those figures, both here and gone,
Who fought for a vision of a brighter dawn
And so she'd strut and so she'd rise
With the wonder of a child's eyes

Though Sara will still perchance a flaw
She has power to leave the world in awe
So in class she raises her arm up high
Like her rainbow bracelet can touch the sky.

RUNNING THROUGH THE FIELDS
BY MAGGIE FALKENBERG

From the first sprouts of green, we start running.
Grass may be plain anywhere else,
but under our feet, it's soft,
and across the hill it rolls in waves,
a sea thousands of miles from the ocean.
The earth is our pillow when our heads fall upon it,
staring up at a brilliantly bright blue sky.
We'll gaze at the clouds and imagine their shapes are
animals and scenes we know.
I'll push you down the side of the hill when we start to
bicker about something stupid,
but it won't take me long to join you,
flipping over and over, smiling like a fool.
You'll probably try and tickle me as pay back
when I land next to you,
and even when I finally get away,
my giggles will continue.

You've told me about a dream with fields of sunflowers,
and I've dreamed it too.
A breeze rustles my dress and the long stems that reach
our heads, as you reach to grab my hand,
joining it with yours, pulling me forward to run.
Run, through a field of tall golden blossoms blessed by
the light of a low setting sun on the horizon.
We'll reach the end of the flower forest
and rest on its edge, looking out upon
the midsummer sunset shining in the west.
I'll say it's the prettiest view I've ever seen in my
experience with sunsets.
You'll return with something cheesy like
"I like the view I have better",
looking at me with your smiling eyes.

Avery Scharf / Frolic Through Freedom

It'll be Fall before we know it, where the leaves start to drift.
The evenings will be cool and quiet,
the only sound our footsteps,
and the moon illuminating the dark shapes of pumpkins.
We don't run, but saunter,
tripping over vines hidden in the shadows we can't see,
fumbling through the patch.
We'll listen to the silence found in autumn,
the rustle of dried leaves under our feet.
I'll shiver from the night's chill,
claiming not to be cold and continuing on.
You'll pull me back, stopping our walk, and wrap your
warm jacket joined by your arms around me.

Snow will then cover those once green hills,
a never ending expanse of white in the distance.
Pure flakes will fall upon our noses and pink rosy faces,
dusting our hair like cotton.
The gray sky will do little to affect our moods,
making the winter day seem like a continuous hour,
counted by our clouds of breath.
We'll dance in the valley we made with our feet,
not traveling far, but swaying to nonexistent music
in our thick coats.
I'll have your mitten in my own, in a cozy grip.
You'll hold it close to your own heart,
promising to never let go.

I HOPE I'D FLY
BY MAGGIE FALKENBERG

I hoped I'd fly
Past all the stars
I would try and try
Yet never get far

My expectations were too great
They'd tell me day after day
I just had to keep my head straight
I would pray and pray

No limitations could stop me
No matter how hard they tried
How hard could it truly be
Goodness my mind lied

It was hard and I failed
The rest saw it ahead
The wall to steep to be scaled
And my dreams entirely shred

Hans Herrera / Specks of Sunlight

BAT POEM
BY MAGGIE FALKENBERG

Oh what a mysterious bird I see
A curious flutter of wings it be
Closer and closer it comes yet
Tipp upon my head sits a fluffy black jet

Its little fangs would barely leave a mark
If they so decided to bite me in the dark
But would such a sweet face do such a deed
I'd say only if it was in true need

This tiny pup looks to the sky
The stars are out up so high
Its eyes flicker with delight
Finding its snack for the night

Away it flys after the bug so quick
Gaining its treat with an even quicker pick
More and more it gains each time
But is eating bugs really such a crime

A small shadow in the light of the moon
The light chirps it starts to croon
Back to its cave it must go
Where it shall await till tomorrow unknown

JUNE
BY MONICA CLARK

Muddy footprints trail behind us
While the inside of your elbow hugs
my cold neck. Limp, your knees pull you
down. You look up at me with apologetic eyes
because even though you asked to walk me,
I still carried you home.

Inside, this house has yet to feel like home.
A tall can split between the two of us.
You laugh at me.
The rough seams on your T-shirt squeezes and hugs
my shoulders, while your eyes
glossy and glazed over watch me laugh with you.

Short, was the amount of time I got to know you
Twisted in bedsheets, your company felt like home
your touch was cautious and gentle, kindness before your eyes
but secrets lingering behind them. I don't know how to define us.
Holding on, those summer memories give my heart warm hugs
Do pop tabs still make you think of me?

Summer memories are all I have to remind me
of what it felt like to be with you
Quiet rooms at parties and suspiciously long hugs
goodbye. In your arms I felt at home.
I wanted more time for us.
More time to look into your eyes.

Brown eyes,
have never looked prettier and everything you showed me
makes it all that much harder to forget us.
Everywhere I go, I think of you.
At night, I wonder if you're at home
missing my goodbye hugs.

At night, when the party gets quiet and she hugs
you goodbye, do you think of me
when you catch a glimpse of her eyes?
And, when your twisted in her bedsheets, do you
feel at home?
Does it ever make you think of us?

NEW YEAR   BY HENRY LAZZARO

The seconds endure
Like the rushing currents of a waterfall
Long before human eyes lay upon them
And long after humans depart from this world

The water will continue to flow
As is has for all time immemorial
Until the final droplet has evaporated from its source
Irrespective of the insignificant emotions of man

Time drags on, slowly, inexorably
11:57, 11:58, 11:59,
Midnight arrives, January the first
Accompanied by a glimmer of hope for what may lie ahead

Hope for newfound prosperity
Hope for strengthened relationships
Hope for exhilarating opportunities
Hope that this year will be better than the last

But all appears unchanged
Nothing about the world surrounding mankind changed
Nothing within man changed
Another tally on the wall of the cell

The changing of the year is meaningless
A mere chimera, a hollow spectacle
Without the will of the individual
To make the forthcoming year better than years past

The water will continue to flow
As it has for all time immemorial
And any man swept under its currents
Will be cast adrift and tossed against the rocky shores below

But still, we cling to hope
For the chance to start anew
To swim against the stream
And embrace the future's endless possibilities

We are the ones who hold the key
To be the masters of our own destiny
And to make this year, and every year,
A time of growth, of love, and of prosperity

So let us resolve to be the change.

A CONVERSATION WITH MY GRANDMA

BY MAX DOMECKA

It wrecked my life
I loved you more than anything
Because you loved me without a cause
But now that you're gone
I feel alone
In a world full of people
So when I saw the stone with your name
Etched so carefully and neatly
And the candle lit shined a glow on the dark stone around you
I couldn't help but cry
Avoiding my look from the stone
Not wanting to show you the tears coming from my eyes
I was not at the ceremony that celebrated your life
Not that I didn't want to go
But there were circumstances, I could not attend
At least I am grateful for that last moment with you
Saying "I love you"
Even if it was an ocean apart
A blue screen between us,
Wishing I knew that it would be my final goodbye

Anthony Colby / Forgotten

ALIEN
BY MAX DOMECKA

A term used against immigrants
A term to make you feel like an outsider

Xenophobia
The hatred of immigrants
Direct or indirect

No one tells you the struggles you face when you're
a child of an immigrant
An immigrant who already had their childhood in
the mother country

Why did we have to leave?

Because when I'm here
I'm too foreign
Too tied to my culture
"Be more American" they say
"Now, you're an American"

I feel like an alien
in a world full of humans

But when I'm home
I'm too westernised
Too American
Or plainly "Američanka"

I'm told to be quiet about my home country
But "we accept everyone"

Do I even have an identity?

Being part of a third culture
Means I can't have a place to call home

A house does not have to be a home
But home is where the heart lives
But what happens when my heart is not accepted

When I feel like
I do not belong
in my country

Standing there
Listening
Knowing
But not understanding

Where are you from?

I say
"Czech Republic"

Oh…
Czechoslovakia?
USSR?

So like,
Russia?

All I want to do is scream
"no … No … NO"

But I can't find that voice
So I say,
"No… just Czech Republic"

They look at me
Confused
But laugh and say,
"Good thing you're here"

As if my country
Was bad

I smile and wave it off
But I can't help but
feel like an outsider
A foreigner
An Alien

GRAY = PURPLE
BY KAYLA MILANO

I love the color purple.
I hate the color gray.
Gray skies,
Gray clouds,
Gray area…
Most of all, I hate gray area.
Not knowing where things stand.
the amount of confusion and anxiety that comes with.
All gray
I hate relationships at this time.
 I hate the way they are solely reliant on phone usage and social media.
 I hate how hard it is to differentiate between a relationship or a "situationship".
They hurt all the same but
Two things that seem so similar can be so different
Relationship definition: "the way in which two or more concepts, objects,
        or people are connected, or the state of being connected."
Situationship definition: "A situationship is that space between a committed
            relationship and something that is more than a friendship,"
When in reality it's just
"relationship with someone who has commitment issues when it's convenient for them"
No more in between
No more gray area
Just black or white
In or out
Left or right
Pick.
Because now I know
I cannot trust the color gray
soon you learn
things get scary
Life gets in the way
They jump ship
And purple fades to gray
Because you lost them all together

Sasha Velazquez / Till Death Do Us Part

EMPTY MIC
BY REGANNE NASH

A few lone souls sit patiently,
as jittering nerves mix in anticipation,
for their turn to express all they've kept hidden.
A time to release thoughts from late at night when no one but the shimmering sky is there for comfort.
One by one, they express their truth, nervous of harsh criticism.
Then...
a wave of support,
from friends...
family...
and strangers unknown,
reassuring their thoughts only recently exposed.
One by one,
as the hand turns round,
feet trickle in
adding to the crowd that started as one.
As the night deepens,
and the audience becomes the cast,
inspiration buds,
connected by the invisible vine,
strung through us all.
One by one, between snaps, cheers, and laughs
suddenly...
a night of courage has faded into a memory.

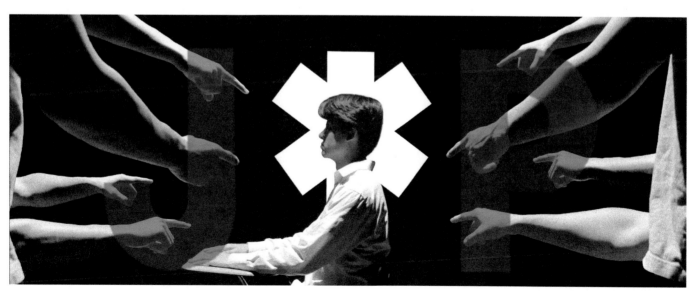

Elijah Nishimura / The Sansei Legacy

STRAWBERRY RHUBARB PIE
BY ADDISON BURNS

I miss Strawberry Rhubarb Pie.

I miss those summers at my Grandparents,
Going out into my grandma's garden to pick her freshly grown rhubarb,
My Papa outside working on some big project,
Like building a deck or installing sprinklers, stuff like that.
I miss feeling the sun on my back,
As I search for the best looking rhubarb,
My little hands getting dirty in the process.

I miss the drive to get the strawberries.
The windows down, wind blowing in my face.
The new car smell that never seemed to go away, no matter how old the car got.
I miss hearing the same story about my Papa catching salamanders when he was a kid,
Every single time we passed his childhood home.
I miss listening to these stories as I watch the blurred horizon,
Imagining I was there catching the salamanders with him.

I miss that busy supermarket,
All the people in their own worlds, all thinking something different.
Being in charge of pushing the cart (which as a 7 year old was a big deal).
Wandering around the bakery section,
Trying to convince my Grandma to get some cookies or a cake.
The loud music blaring over the speakers, almost too loud.
All while praying we'll go out for lunch after.

I miss the trip to the pie store to get the crust,
The feeling of the cold crust straight from the freezer,
The smell of freshly baked pies,
Getting to try any flavor of pie I'd like.
It was like heaven for a 7 year old.

I miss getting back to my grandma's house and immediately making the pie.
I miss my Papa sleeping in his chair while my grandma and I rolled out the crust.
I miss being able to pour the sugar into the bowl,
I always felt so important when I did that.
Waiting till after dinner to try the pie was agonizing,
Seeing it on the counter and smelling it,
It was so tempting.
I miss my Papa taking the first bite and going on and on about how great it was,
Telling us it was the best pie he ever had.
That feeling of proudness I got seeing my Papa enjoy the pie (that I made!) made me feel so cool.

I miss that strawberry rhubarb pie.

TOXIC PASTA
BY MADDIE WETLE

Giggles of excitement as we grocery shop.
A spectacular date night.
I imagined us in my kitchen,
a scene out of a Hallmark movie.
Frank Sinatra echoes around the candle lit house.

Creamy tomato pasta.
A five ingredient dish.
Seems simple enough.
 Simple was not a word in our vocabulary.
Everything was a challenge.

Three clicks and the stove was lit.
The tomatoes were in preparation first.
He didn't like the way I cut tomatoes.
Instead, I was given the sous chef honor of retrieving a box of pasta noodles.
I threw fresh basil into the assortment of tomatoes, cream, and spices.
The pan whooshes up in crackling smoke.
Garlic and red pepper flakes emit a familiar sting.

Instead of kisses, we shared words.
 Soon enough, I felt as obliterated as the cherry tomatoes,
Deflating in the pan.

The water is boiling.
Salad preparation turned into a police interrogation.
We are just hungry, let's finish this.
The water is boiling.
"I don't like when you"
The water is boiling.
"Why do you always"
The water is boiling
"Do you even care about"
The water is boiling.
He is boiling over.

The first bite was going to fix it all.
Soon enough, our stomachs were full.
We did what we knew best, temporary satisfactions,
Temporary fixes.
But we're both hungry again.

Yesterday I made creamy tomato pasta.
It had been more than a year.
I had Frank Sinatra on full volume.
The aroma was better than I remembered.
I prepared everything myself.
I cut the tomatoes with precision and confidence.
The water didn't boil over.
I sat, fork in hand with a shaky smile.

I was full.
I hope wherever he is now, he is too.

Zoe Price / Stringless

92 DAYS
BY MATTHEW ATLAS

3
months since you told me you'd keep your eye on
me

92
days between that moment and the moment you
started watching me from above

2,208
hours fill the space between that last conversation
and the day you changed our lives so drastically

132,480
minutes between that last text and your last exhale

2,119,680
breaths made all the difference

1
uncle that changed my life

ROOFTOP
BY KRISTOPHER SMITH

And thus, so the sun did set;
Dimmed, the pillars of song and light
Along the birches, far and near
Above the trees, so everclear
The poet and the muse had rambled off
And so, just did, the jesters and dove

REBORN
BY KRISTOPHER SMITH

(New Year)
Is here, my clock rambles on
My oblivion minus one, my escape forgone
A tower slowly winks, and with each and every wink
The encroaching mist ensures its veil

Rain pouring down rimes this body, and near
With cloud cloaking my mind, I stand with drear
It's mist remains quiet, in front, to rear
I stand steadfast, I have something to fear

The hour groweth short on a life shortly lived
Yet to bring fourth reprieve, (or) revival
My hour grows late, yet the time never too late
To tack this ship from steer through the strait

Twenty three'll be no different, twenty two, nor
twenty one
Until the change that beset the melancholy, rise like
the sun
I peer at the rhythmic blink, the tower slowly winks
The ascent, I begin, in these final persist(s)

With each and every grasp, I hold and belate
For just one mistake, I seal my fate
Higher and higher, the fog ran thin and thin
Leaving me evermore filled, wit overmost vim

"One after one by the star dogged moon…"
I climb these poles to above smoke and doom
Above chaos, lied a heaven unseen
Above the chaos, I felt evermost free

Time will tell how long I fought
With stroke of the pen, I hurry and jot
A return to surface, I jump into doom
I fall downwards, then up, the flower has bloomed

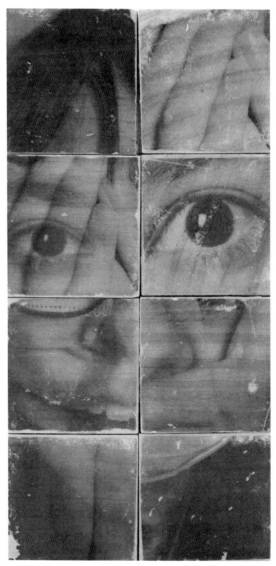

Jessica Nakayama / ReBuilt

I AM FROM.
BY NIA ELLIS

I am from the unrealistic beauty standards of America.
I am thirsting for the validation of being beautiful.
I crave acceptance from those who I aspire to be.
In reality I know because of who I am, I can not be.
Hours of indulging in the toxicity that Instagram sets out to be
Kardashians all over my feed.

Do you know what this does to a young girl who looks like me?
From a world who competes with girls for beauty standards
I'll never be able to achieve
Insecure.
Wish my nose was slimmer
Rhinoplasty searched on twitter
Wish I was confident.
I am just incompetent

Wish I didn't look like me
I'm supposed to be perfect you see?
Reminiscing over love songs on the radio

Oh, I wish you would feel that way towards me.
I am stuck in jealousy and rage
Topped off with pity and shame
I am from a place of sorrow and hurt.

A bundle of anxiety
from a place of sobriety
I just want to be enough.
Was this written for me up above?

I am from a place of dysfunction and anger
stemming from a dad who couldn't show me love until way later.
I am a young teen who only wants to be seen.
Why must America make these standards so different from you and me?

HALLS
BY CHRISTIAN CARTER

As I grace these halls, it feels like a sprinkler.
Glistening me in the beautiful memories that one can experience.
That one time I fell in the crowd or even when I saw my photo on the wall.
Time might have been limited, but what a short journey, nonetheless.
Pacing back and forth, reflecting on the years that once felt so comfortable.

However, it never stays relatively the same, does it?
A haunting memory these halls hold.
A snow globe that you can hold and cherish but can never be a part of.
If time stopped for just one moment, I'd sit down and stare out the window,
wondering why the world has to carry on.

The world is a dangerous place where the unknown is, well, unknown.
No answer sheet, no guide, no way of knowing where you might go.
Stuck on an abandoned road where no one is following you.
Trapped in a maze where the exit is nonexistent.
Existing in nothingness, no surroundings, no noise, nothing.

But maybe that's the beauty in it.
There's attractiveness in the unknown as the future isn't set in stone.
You can do whatever you choose and do it well in life.
Brew coffee, travel the world, or just sit at home.
If the future is unknown, then let it stay that way.

MANGOES.
BY FALIHA KHAN

I remember long limb trees,
With large orange-yellow pieces of treasure,
Hanging just within reach,
Next to the balcony of my mother's childhood home in India.

I remember picking the fresh fruit,
Hearing the satisfactory snap as it detached itself from the bending tree.
Carefully holding on to its cool oval shaped exterior,
Our basket filled to the brim with this sweet tropical fruit,
Much like the overfilled joy reflected through our bright smiles and awestruck expressions.

I remember my cousins and I watching in anticipation,
As our grandmother carefully cut the mangoes in perfect square shaped pieces,
Almost tasting the faint scent of its saccharine goodness.

I remember the unforgettable first taste,
Savoring the explosion of the sweet sugary juice that came with every bite,
The soft inside that contrasted its hard surface.
It's nostalgic recalling the constant laughter and carefree conversations,
That took place over a small bowl of this healing fruit.

I remember visiting India with my family every few years,
As each visit was welcomed with hugs and a bowl of mangoes,
Freshly picked from right outside our house,
A building that was present in all of our lives.

But cheerful memories often turn sour,
When these jovial events cease to occur,
And the mangoes are simply a stinging reminder
Of a heartfelt family tradition that was taken from you.

The sweet juice becomes bitter to the taste,
The soft inside is now similar to its hard surface,
And the long limb trees no longer provide
the large orange-yellow pieces of treasure.

The memory-filled walls
Of my mother's childhood home
Are simply a remnant of my reminiscences.
My grandmother is no longer there
To cut the fruit into perfect square shaped pieces,
And the mangoes that were once attached to feelings of whole-heartedness joy
Are now a hollow reminder of the absences that truly gave it meaning.

THE DECAY OF EDEN : MY LAST BREATH
BY SANA MUNEER

My rotting body decays in the greenery
Parched skin crushing the blades beneath
Flowers grow like weeds from my failing arteries,
Decorating me like a wreath

Blooming from my blood
Yet shriveling to the kiss of burnt air
Petals fall in dozens
Laying to rest in my hair

Sun spots disappear
Once splattered across my cheeks
A forest of freckles falls
What once stood tall, now weak

Scars jagged across my arms
Where an expanse of mountains reign
Blood seeps through the cracks
White peaks red with pain

A reflection wavers in the storm
Bruised birthmarks begin to fade
A weary soul unravels in waves
And history washes away

My creations rise to meet each other
In a fruitless dance of conquest
These hands are not the ones I know
I am surrendering now to rest

Looking up above
The sky whispers its pleas
Beckoning me to save it
As humans sink to their knees

Your arrogance burns me
And your world crumbles beyond repair
How can you not hear?
I've been screaming to the air

A soul turned to ash
Endless chances sacrificed for pleasure
Futile attempts to save me
In the end, there was no good measure

Hans Herrera / Do/Not Belong Together

TWINLESS
BY SANA MUNEER

Everywhere I look, there are two.
Two of my mom's smiles.
Two of my dad's noses.
Two sets of my grandmother's doting eyes.

My mom: a twin.
My dad: a twin.
My grandmother: a twin.
I constantly see double.

As a curious child who never felt whole, I wondered where my twin went.
Adventuring through magical worlds, I filled the gaps with fictional characters
I found myself reflected in the ocean of literature.

I cultivated my identity, not through shared double traits,
But through discovering myself in what I loved.

I realized I don't need another half to be whole.

Elijah Nishimura / Untitled

THE TREE
BY CHRISTIAN CARTER

Since the moment the tree was created, the leaf stood alongside the tree.
The tree and the leaf grew together, one and the same, connected by only a single twig.
But that twig, so strong, could last them through the spring
and nothing would take that away.

The leaf, throughout the year, changes, and isn't the leaf that the tree once knew.
The leaf's color shifts from green into amber and bronze, wishing for life on the ground.
A wish that would mean that the two would be separated.
The tree can do nothing but stand there and hope the wish doesn't come true.

As seasons pass and piercing chill fills the air, the leaf can no longer hold on.
It lets go of the tree, of the memories that they shared.
The tree wonders why time goes by so fast, wondering why their time was short.
As the leaf falls to a new beginning, the tree stays in place.

Days go by without the tree's friend and the tree realizes that the other leaves have started to fall.
The tree wanted to find any resemblance to the past that excited its branches.
It stands alone, stripped of everything that the tree knew.
Ashamed that now, it has to face its fears alone.

The tree wastes its time waiting for the leaf to return, for anyone to come back.
But they never do, not even while they're clearly in front of them.
A friendship is supposed to be a two-player game, not a one-man show.
All those memories, those glimpses of happiness, crumble in front of the tree's stump.

But the flowers start to bloom, the tree starts to grow its color back,
and new leaves start to form on the tree.
Thus, another cycle begins, continuing until the end of time.
More leaves to meet and more leaves to leave

MY STORY
BY CHRISTIAN CARTER

4 people: grandparents.
They all have stories to tell, they all have
siblings to share them with, and they all have
tens of cousins to joke around with.

2 people: parents.
Less stories to tell, less siblings to share their
stories with, less cousins joke around with,
but they have each other to listen.

1 person: me
I have no siblings to share my stories with,
barely any cousins to talk, let alone play with
But it's still my story.
Nothing can take my story away and even
though it's just a couple of chapters in a Leo
Toystol-esque book, it's mine to tell, mine to
share, mine to joke.

0 people: my kids
My story might not even be passed along
once I'm gone.
No kids to scare, to excite, to inspire, just
simple sentences in a lost notebook.

But my story will only live on from the
people I trust, my story will only live through
the photos I take. My story is mine.

Elise Fey / Beneath The Surface

WHERE I'M FROM
BY FELICITY ABBOTT

I am from the town of lilacs
The town rich with history
And thick with the blooming florals

I am from the lilac parade
Passing by the mayor's pizza shop
And the lilac princess ice cream floats

I am from the choo-choo restaurant
With its vanilla cupcakes topped with
Birthday train whistles and sprinkles
from the train baskets that brought my grilled cheese
And the grandparents who celebrated with me

I am from yelling at my sister
For tripping me on the carpet

I am from my dad's camcorder
Interviewing me before every first day of school
From the same camcorder I use
To film my last year of school

I am from wishing I was Hannah Montana
And memorizing her songs
And watching her show late at night

I am from California Girls, Disturbia
and Kidz Bop music videos
And from never knowing the correct lyrics

I am from Freaky Friday
And Lindsey Lohan playing her red bass
Wearing her shirt inside out

I am from Sweet and Sassy birthday parties
Fully equipped with my Brittney Spears headset
And doused in every glitter imaginable
The scent of artificial fruit and candy
clinging to the air and hairspray

6_1

I am from falling asleep in the car
Letting the sound of the road lull me to sleep

I am from 4th of July parties
Running after fireflies and
Watching fireworks from the highway

I am from a place of silly little traditions
Made up by us
Secrets and inside jokes shared by family

I am from home

I AM FROM DREAMS
BY LIZZIE STEELE

I am from runs to the park,
I am from make believe games,
I am from dreaming I'm a princess,
I am from believing I'm brave.

I am from dreams that pass,
Without a second gaze.
Looking in mirrors,
Seeing a different self.

I am from reality,
That never seems to settle.
I am from anywhere but here,
But my location stays the same.

I am from the games never played,
Toys left on a shelf for another day.
I am from believing they're real,
With the empty space they take.

I am from summer days taking long,
The sun never set
I am from friends for forever,
You always knew what to say.

I am from growing older by the day,
I am from dreams left behind,
I am from realizations of reality,
I am from grief of the dreams we once thought was real.

Erik Schmall / Window Pane

Short Fiction.

INNOCENT WINTER   BY MAGGIE FALKENBERG

White hills glisten in the late evening snow. The dark shadows of houses and other buildings dot the valley with imperfections. Light powder will cover them soon, similarly dusting a black woolen coat upon the highest slope.

The figure of a man leans on the front of a sleek car, so slick it repels any frost wanting to creep across its shine. He looks down into the frozen village, quiet in the night, seconds passing as each flurry falls.

A world below and beyond at peace once more after six years, yet so many hearts among them are still at war. The timer ticks away, his duty to disrupt the peace encroaching on his mind. He just needed a moment. A moment to see, a moment to wonder, and a moment to remember.

His hometown doesn't feel like home anymore.

…

The front window is blurred, a battleground between the inner warmth and outer cold. Woken from bed, a young woman sits staring out through the fogginess into an empty street. Was it a bad dream that woke her? A sad and lonely feeling? She can't recall, but her uneasiness had yet to settle.

Every so often a shiver sends her sleepy eyes open again, stopping their resumption of sleep. It isn't cold in the humble parlor, but the slight chill from the window crack makes every part of her body, but her mind, languid and frozen. Her daze is only broken when headlights flash onto the street, curving around the corner till they shine across the yard.

…

He knows the layout of the town by heart. The park with the little lake and the corner home to the tall evergreen tree. He remembers the diner as the grand retreat. The red stools they would sit on after school as teenagers, on the weekends. The sweet frozen desserts they would stir and spoon.

There's the hospital at the end of the street. An unremarkable building of age that housed the people he loved. The church sits on the hill on the other side, where prayers went unanswered. His mother and father are buried next to each other there, forever a part of the town they never escaped.

At least he had made it out. Even if it meant missing the funeral and a last goodbye.

…

The sirens haven't gone off in months, the eeriness in their absence still a novelty. Radios no longer report updates and the advances of the Allies. They're no longer under a blackout order from the military. They're safe.

Away from harm as they've always been. Still idling, only watching. That quietness leads to waiting. That waiting leads to thought.

It was early on in her life that the woman realized not many left or came to her hometown, nestled between the hills, obscure from all relevance. The need for change takes over one's mind till the pressure to submit to the daily town life vanquishes any inkling of a dream.

She had a dream once. To run away to a bustling world where sitting and waiting wasn't even an option. To explore the world with a friend, rather than just adventuring through the park along the lake. Yet then a war broke out, separating the world into two sides, and a child's dream became irrelevant. It seemed people finally left their little hills. Her father, her neighbors, her adventurous friend.

A chance was given to him. All she wanted for once in her life was for him to choose their town. To stay rooted next to where, she too, was stuck. She had looked into his eyes, filled with the green of the hills that surrounded them, and pleaded. His roots held too much pain to keep though, and he left. He volunteered the day he turned eighteen, was given a gun, and shipped off.
She was left behind in their lonely town, only wanting to follow him to the front, but doomed to stay home waiting.

…

He avoids passing his childhood home, instead heading to the other side of town. He turns the corner, snow grinding under his tires. A familiar house sits on the cul de sac, the car's lights illuminating the white specks as they fall onto the yard.

The front door stands stoic and still, awaiting his action. It takes him a moment to rest his knuckles on the painted wood, chills running up and down his arm. Perhaps he needs a new coat, he thinks, though the rest of his body is perfectly warm.

Finally, a light tap breaks the streets silence.

…

She hears a soft knock sound from her door.

There's nothing for a moment. Then another slightly stronger, more insistent knock, echoes from the hall.

The woman had seen the car pull into her driveway, the dark figure emerge and walk the steps. She tries to suppress it, but hope takes a grip of her mind. It's slim and slight, but it makes her rise to her feet and approach the door. She takes the door handle, turns the lock, and opens her house to the biting night.

…

He looks at the girl, now a woman he'd known since they were children playing in the park. He watches a shudder run through her as tears form in her eyes. He knows she wants to scream at him for coming back. Afterall, he'd left. He'd left them both, but he wasn't there to apologize. It was too late for that.

No. He had news to tell her, but he was almost certain she already knew. Tonight was just supposed to be a delivery. He didn't have the time to dwell on it, or his own tears would start to form and freeze across his cheeks. He doesn't want to remember she's not the only one who lost him.

…

"He's gone," The man says.

She looks at the man that succeeded in escaping. He made it back alive, but her friend, and his younger brother, wouldn't be coming back. Not to her. Not to him. Not even to this town. He made a risk to escape, and it cost the ultimate price.

STARS, MCDONALD'S AND SHOES
BY FELICITY ABBOTT

Every night that summer, we met on that old McDonald's roof. Every night that summer we gazed at the stars. Every night that summer my converse tapped to the sound of your guitar. Every night that summer we lived. We lived with reckless abandon, always speeding down dark streets with our loud music. We celebrated just the fact that we were alive. Remember that one night at our McDonald's? The one where the cops came and we hid. I thought the squeak of my shoes would give us away. Boy, was my dad mad. He grounded me for weeks. That didn't stop us from sneaking out. While my dad thought I was sleeping, we were hanging out in loud dark basements clouded with sweat and cologne. While my dad thought I was reading, we were riding the rickety Ferris wheel at the county fairgrounds. That summer we were everywhere doing almost everything and nothing at the same time. We felt untouchable and our love felt real.

Now, the magic from that summer and the summers after seems to have faded. We're lucky to even eat dinner together with the kids. You're always working late while I work at home to keep our family moving forward. When you come home with your tie loosened and your hair messy, I look into your eyes but I no longer see the spark of the boy that I fell in love with so many years ago. My heart yearns for the excitement we had that one summer. My eyes wish to look at the world wide and innocently like we did that one summer. My ears strain to hear the long forgotten song of your guitar that you played that one summer. I still remember every day of that summer. These days bleed together, the same lonely routine after the other. I'm tired of living on a loop.

I hope while you're reading this, you can understand my point of view. I hope you find this note before you find your house empty. I've left you all of your belongings, they don't mean much to me anymore. I've taken the children, they don't benefit from an absent father. Maybe one day we'll see each other again from across the street. And maybe you'll remember that one summer and the love we once had for each other. And in that moment, you'll realize no matter how much you once loved someone, that doesn't guarantee their love in the present. I truly wish the best for you and hope you can rediscover your happiness.

Kathy Georgieva / Untitled

THE VISIT
BY KRISTOPHER SMITH

I step through the door. I am greeted by the same obtrusive green carpet that had been laid long before my arrival to life. A sense of familiarity washes over me as I am greeted by the quaint scent of the house, a scent no other home I had visited had floating in its air. I walk deeper into the room, my silhouette shadows the floor and wall I stand in front of. The pictures that had once been, no longer hang in their original positions they took place long ago. Instead, they appear absent, revealing that the wall is no longer the same mint green it had been originally. Funny how your imagination fills in the blanks, almost as if the wall had always been the same red that it is now.

I looked to my left seeing the same staircases that had led both up and downstairs: the stairs on the left went down, and the stairs on the right led to the upstairs. The brown rail guards that my grandfather had put up still stood, untouched. However the eyesore of the untuned, filthy, organ my grandma had barely used had not been there either, much alike to the paintings. Neither was the cabinet filled with all of her random art that stood on the right-side of the organ. The dining room table had appeared unchanged, but the room was too dark for me to see. I had wanted to go upstairs to look around, but I couldn't bring myself to the task, something felt off.

Out of what I could make of the darkness at the top of the steps, the master-bedroom door swung open. A younger looking man had stepped into the hallway: my grandpa's office to his left; in front of the doorway leading into the master bedroom. Behind him, was the door to my mother and her siblings' old room. To the man's immediate right; my left, was the door to the bathroom, which also had a doorway leading into the bedroom as well. There was a fear that had clouded the space that took between me and the guy, I couldn't tell if it was my heart that I was hearing beat, or his.

Twelve steps up, the guy had finally mustered the courage to ask: "what are you doing here?". His voice was soft and shaky, this was obviously his first time. A person from looks of it - his wife, had come out into the hallway that led into the four other rooms, and the closet that stood in front of the bathroom door: she stood behind his right shoulder; the left for me. One thing was clear, two elephants stood in an empty warehouse, the two on top of the stairs were intruding in my grandparents home; or my grandparents had no longer lived here, due to the fact of them being long dead. I stood at the bottom of the steps as I turned to look into the kitchen, I was looking to see if anything had changed.

A low blue hue came from what looked to be a stove, had reflected off of the floor and ceiling, the blue numbers read "4:51". I could feel the light from my car that shone through the front window pour over my body, as I slowly turned my head back towards him. I cocked my head to my right shoulder, just like how I do it every time this happens. Something, however, had caught my eye. It was that old-extra dining room table chair that sat to the right of the steps, just like it had my last visit. I couldn't break eye contact with the chair, almost as if I were under a spell. My grandma would sometimes sit in it before her passing, or others, including myself at times, would use it as a place to rest their coats upon coming to visit. I looked back to the two to see both, my grandma and grandpa standing at the top of the steps.

The golden late-afternoon sunset poured through the window behind me. Between two mint green walls, there stood, both, my grandma and grandpa. All of this had felt too familiar. I now felt comfortable moving up the stairs. When I reached the top of the steps I embraced my grandma with a long, warm hug, she laughed along with my grandpa. Everything had been perfect just like before, same as it ever was . . .

EXPIRATION DATE   BY FELICITY ABBOTT

Everyone has an expiration date. Everyone knows that. It's hard to forget when it's permanently stamped to your arm. A constant reminder that life isn't infinite. What no one knows is what happens after. Expireds seem to just disappear and after a while, it becomes harder and harder to remember who vanished.

There are schoolyard theories of what happens to those who expire; they burst into flames and disintegrate, and other crude stories of death. The children are smart enough to tell these tales in hushed tones. Someone is always listening and they don't like it when we ask questions. A good citizen is one that lives a good unquestioning life and accepts expiration. Every United Commonwealth citizen knows the official reason given for expiration dates: To preserve our resources, stimulate innovation, and perpetuate progressive ideals. However, after somehow becoming the only one in your family unexpired, you start to wonder the purpose of it all.

Most people's expiration dates are between 25-40. Your expiration date is always the day after your birthday. That way you can celebrate your last day with your family and friends and vanish with a stomach full of birthday cake. At least, that's what I've always imagined. My 20th birthday is tomorrow, and the day after is my expiration date. I expire a lot sooner than most, but I'm not scared. I'm ready. I have no family anymore. I obviously had to have had a mom and dad at one point, but I've long forgotten everything about them. I had a brother though. His expiration date was last year after his 27th birthday. I've already forgotten his name and the way he looked.

I look in the mirror at my sparkly party dress. I picked it out several years ago with, I assume, my mom in preparation for this day. I tighten one of the straps then decide I look good enough.

My friends are throwing my last birthday party and I'm actually really excited. I put Sophie in charge since she's known for her extravagant party planning. From what I've heard from others, she's organized several meal courses, invited nearly half the town, and hired a live band.

I fiddle with my hair for a few minutes before giving up. No one will remember what I looked like in a few weeks anyways.

When I arrive at Sophie's apartment I'm immediately overwhelmed by the amount of people, food and sound. Sophie squeals and throws her arms around me. She takes my hand and leads me into the living room where she stands on the coffee table, raises her champagne glass and gives an elaborate toast only Sophie would come up with.

The rest of the night was a blur of stuffing my face with french pastries, dancing and saying goodbye. There were a few tears shed, but overall the night was very festive.

I walked home wine drunk and happy. I breathed in the crisp night air and looked up at the stars one last time. When I got home, I took my time getting ready for bed. As I entered my room, I let out a sigh knowing I would never see it again. I gently hung up my dress in my closet, hoping that someone someday will be able to wear it.

I put on my most comfortable pajamas and slide into my covers. I let myself succumb to sleep and say goodbye to the world.

***

I startle awake to the sound of a blaring alarm. I sit up and immediately regret it. My head feels like it's stuffed with cotton and my limbs are heavy.

I look down and I'm no longer wearing my pajamas, but a hospital gown two sizes too big is haphazardly tied around my body.

I have several needles in my arms with various mysterious liquids coming to and from. I'm about to cry out for help when I hear a cold robotic voice come over the intercom.

"Hello. Welcome to Project EXP."

And before I could process what I was going on, the world was enveloped in darkness.

ACTIONS HAVE CONSEQUENCES
BY CHRISTIAN CARTER

Resting on his bed lay Terrence, mind completely free of thought. Lofi music filled his ears, his headphones blasting at total volume. He stared mindlessly at the ceiling, noticing the bumps and counting them individually. The world seemed so more prominent than what he once thought it was. He was now an adult but still felt like a little kid no matter where he went. He had social anxiety, and whenever someone would talk to him, he would stutter his words until he found it helpful not to say anything. College certainly didn't help with his way of thinking, as he stayed to himself in his dorm room, even avoiding talks with his roommate as much as he possibly could. Fortunately, his roommate was friendly and spent time with others, leaving Terrence to relax in his dorm, free from the worry of social contact.

To remedy his situation, he refocused his attention from the ceiling on his phone and to find some sort of entertainment. He scrolled through it, page after page until he landed on Instagram. Although he could barely hold a conversation, he did have people back home whom he felt comfortable enough to call friends. He had some friends at the photography club with whom he had spent time on a few occasions and began to stalk them lightly. The first "victim" was Levi, whose profile was filled with photos at his new school. 'He looked so happy,' Terrence thought, and a slight smile formed. The second one was Kai, someone he'd been friends with for well over six years. Their page had been left untouched, but from what he last heard, they were traveling the world with their family. A tear fell onto his cheek, happy at the fact that his friends were moving on but upset that his life was mediocre. After scrolling through his friend's media for what seemed hours, he ended up on his friend Max's Instagram page.

She had an Instagram story, and when he saw it, his phone slipped from his hand onto his stomach. He frantically picked up the phone and reopened the account in disbelief. Did he really just see that? He clicked on the post, and his mouth dropped all through the nine circles of hell. An image of a graffitied sign saying the phrase, '@%&# your authority.' The sign that he worked day in and day out to raise money for. The sign that commemorated his very friend that the sign was meant for.

His mind flashed back to the very day of the accident. He was sitting in the back seat of his friend's car, staring out the open window at the sunset. He stuck his head out, felt the smooth breeze splash his face with nothing but happy thoughts, and closed his eyes, hoping the moment would never end. Terrence and his friends were on their way to the beach, a day they had planned for the last month. They had all requested days off of their work to experience the water before they had to leave for college. His friend, Taylor, sat shotgun in the car, foot tapping to the blaring sound of rock music. He could still picture her outfit even to this day. A black tennis skirt and baggy long-sleeved shirt dressed her body paired with combat boots and sunglasses. He only spent a few times on the car ride looking over at her, at any of his friends. He spent most of his time pondering the future choices he'll eventually make while looking out at the nature surrounding him. He didn't truly experience the beauty of the trees and the flora because suddenly, his head smashed into the seat before him, and he blacked out.

Terrence opened his eyes slightly and peered around. This wasn't his friend's car. Shouldn't they have made it to the beach already? Why was he unconscious, and why was the last thing he remembered being thrust into the seat? After analyzing his surroundings, he took notice of the people that were moving around him. They wore all-white clothes, and it felt like Terrence was being ascended into the heavens by a flock of angels. The feeling of cool metal chilled his entire body and made him question what was happening even more than before. He opened his mouth to speak but found it difficult to form a coherent sentence and closed it. He could hear the people around him saying words, and from what he saw, they were speaking to him, yet when he tried to listen, all he heard was muffled conversation. The people brought Terrence into a van, which terrified the boy, and he attempted to fight them back. He was quickly detained by them and slowly started to drift out of consciousness. Terrence could hear voices, and even thought one of them said, 'Stay awake for me,' but he couldn't resist the urge and gave in.

He woke up later that day and found out what had happened. According to his parents, a truck ran a red light and crashed head-on into his friend's car, which was why Terrence couldn't remember anything that had happened. He only suffered whiplash and a concussion from his head being positioned right by the car seat in front of him. Jamie, Terrence's friend in the back seat with him, suffered minor injuries, most of which were a couple of bruises and whiplash. Roxy, who was driving the car, was hospitalized for many days from her injuries. She had a broken nose, leg, and many scratches, some requiring stitching. Terrence asked about Taylor following the travesty of his other friends; however, his parents stayed silent. Terrence asked again to no response. His parents bursted into tears, and after the long pauses of silence, Terrence already knew what had happened to his dear friend.

The news spread around the community quickly, and they were in shock. Taylor had always been such a sweet and humble girl, and no one could fathom the idea that she would no longer be in their lives. Funds were sent to her family to cover funeral expenses, and memorials popped up around her school. But it didn't feel enough. Taylor's life was worth more than some money and a couple of photos surrounding a dozen candles. The students lobbied together to replace the school sign in memory of Taylor so that it would be like she never left. Administrators appreciated the students' efforts working together for a common cause and agreed to fund part of it. Although the new sign was expensive, it was worth every penny. Terrence had been at the forefront of the movement and picked up extra

shifts at the restaurant to pay for the sign. He put his blood, sweat, and tears into ensuring the legacy of his late friend was sustained for the years to come. Even though four people entered that car and three people left, Taylor's impact on everyone would be remembered.

Terrence came to his senses and returned to the present day, wheezing and coughing from the shock of seeing the post. He felt angry that one of the only ways his friend was remembered by society had been tarnished by people that wanted to act cool to their friends. But on the other hand, he couldn't blame them for acting like teenagers, and he didn't want to. The biggest question on his mind was how Max could do that to him. She had known that Taylor was one of Terrence's closest friends. She knew that the loss affected him deeply. She knew that he had worked hard and long to pay for the cost of the sign, but she didn't care about any of that. He knew she couldn't get away with this, and her friends couldn't. He got onto his laptop and looked up the principal's email account from his high school. He carefully wrote down every word he said to maximize the effect they would have on her. He grabbed the picture Max had shared, copied it into the email, and sent it.

His head aggressively fell onto the pillow, and he continued to gaze at the ceiling while reflecting on the situation. Was it the right thing to do? Should he not have said anything? Someone would've found out eventually; he just made it happen faster. God, if Taylor were still around, she would call him a snitch. But it didn't matter to him. What mattered was that his friend's name shouldn't have been disrespected, and the sign devoted to her should have never been touched. He missed her like crazy, and sometimes while he was asleep, he'd imagine that she was still here, and like most of those days, he dozed off, thinking about her with a smile.

Personal Essay.

KHANDAAN
BY ANEEQA MEAH

My family speaks four different languages.

They can speak English and Burmese.

The majority of my family lived and grew up in Myanmar, with the exception of the newer generation. Ammi grew up there, Abba grew up there. I did not grow up there because by the time I was born, my parents had traveled across the world to America. They had moved in a quaint neighborhood where much of my extended family had made lives for themselves since their own arrivals to America.

But despite the new country, new customs, and (almost) new language, my family never lost their culture. I grew up around parents always speaking in a familiar but mostly incomprehensible language with each other that I later grew to understand more and more. Saturdays were reserved for Burmese dishes like Mohinga (wheat noodles in fish soup), Ohn-no-khao-swe (wheat noodles in curried chicken and coconut milk broth), and my favorite, Laphet thoke (tea leaf salad). I'd always see my Abba lazing around in his maroon lungi on his days off from work, and often wondered how he managed to wrap it so that it wouldn't fall. My Ammi would often crave a certain sweet in the morning and by the afternoon, it would be made and in the fridge wrapped up in foil or in a jug filled with ice.

The overall uniqueness of it all is what I love most. There is no culture like this, and I love telling people that my favorite thing to eat is tea leaf salad and that the best skincare routine that's worked for me is crushed root paste and that the velvet Mandalay chappal with the silver designs are the comfiest footwear I've ever owned.

Gujarati is an addition to the languages.

My khandaan, or lineage, leads back to India—specifically the city of Surat. I'm not too connected with this part of myself, however my family mostly communicates with each other in Gujarati.

We still make the occasional Surti sweets and Bollywood movies have always been a big part of my life.

I didn't find out I was part Indian until a few years ago, though it wasn't too hard to believe. I'd already recognized myself with the South Asian community and knew that was where I also fit.

For some reason, they can also speak Urdu.

Weirdly enough, I'm more connected with my Pakistani culture than I am with my Indian heritage. It's impossible for me to determine where Pakistan was thrown into the mix - since my ancestors originated from India- but I'm just as much involved in this culture as I am with my Burmese heritage. Urdu was my first language, and Fridays were meant for shalwar kameez and choosing Pakistani dramas over Disney movies as a child.

And the most important thing that this culture has taught me is the value of family. Despite the flaws and fights that come from them, we are all very involved in each other's lives, but just enough to respect each other's boundaries.

And because of this proximity, I grew up with my culture infused in me through them (in the vice versa sort of way). We'd have the occasional family gatherings, where we'd only have to walk a few blocks to get to anyone's house. There'd be a plethora of languages being spoken, with the elders speaking in Gujarati and Urdu, the younger kids talking in English, and quiet Burmese spoken with gossip here and there, indicating that secrets were being exchanged. And someone always chipped in to make a traditional dish, even if there were already plans to order out.

This mix of all these different influences has been what I've always known and what has made me into me. Being surrounded by my family and what they represent has always felt like home.It has always been where I've been the happiest.

ON THE MOUND
BY FRANKY VALLI

The Iowa sun continues its assault on me as I walk to the mound. I wipe the pine tar off of my hands and pick up the ball from the scorching turf. After what seemed like a hundred warmup pitches, the batter stepped in. I lean in, looking for the sign from my catcher: fastball. I wind up and let go, the rough seams ripping off my fingertips. Crack! The ball sails toward centerfield. My fielder is outlined against the corn as he makes the catch. This was turning out to be a memorable end to my travel baseball career.

Misto 1

VICTORY!
BY CHLOE SCHMIDT

My cheer team entered the warm up area with the uncertainty of what would happen in the room right next to us. We all breathed heavily. My hands were saturated with sweat, and my heart was racing. All I could think about was falling short of first place last year all because of my stunt collapsing. With this thought, we walked onto the mat. The music began thumping along with the beat of my heart. Perfect beats led to a perfect routine. The next time we walked back into the gym for awards, we walked out with the biggest trophy.

WILLOW TREES
BY GRACE GEIMER

When my dad and I arrived at our secret place, we hid our bikes behind a tall bush. Branches on willow trees hung low and brushed the tall, uncut grass. We held onto the strong, flexible arms of the trees and swung for what felt like hours. The smell of grass and clean air hit me with every gust of warm wind. The only sound that broke the beautiful quiet of birds chirping and leaves rustling was the laughter of 8 year old me. When life gets heavy, my mind takes me back to the willow trees.

BLUE EYES
BY KADEN KU

He slouches in his chair leaning into the palm of his hand, waiting for the voice to begin his long day ahead. Until he notices the girl sitting in the row before him. He sits upright in his chair and feels himself drawn in her direction. He stares in awe as she makes conversation with a friend. He interrupts to introduce himself. She turns to him and he catches a glimpse of her deep, blue eyes, as she gives him a warm inviting smile. Before he can say anything more, the professor walks in and so begins their day ahead.

RUNNERS TAKE YOUR MARKS
BY JACOB LICHTENHELD

I can still remember the chill running down my spine as the runners lined up by their schools. The piercing shot from the gun erupted, starting total chaos for the first few seconds of the race. What seemed like hundreds of running shoes clouded my vision until everyone finally began to spread apart. I realized that I was in second place, with first not far ahead. By the last hundred meters of an excruciating two-mile run, my legs were on fire and my brain demanded that I stop. But I overcame my internal struggle, taking first by a mere half-second.

STALL FOR TIME   BY DANIEL BARATKA

9..10..11..12..13 the clock ticked, second after second like an occasional breeze it made a slightly louder tick every minute. Then it would start again, the hand creeping around the small circular clock, dancing around the roman numerals. When the longer hand hit the 12 I'd always hope for it to freeze and never move again, but as always the ticking would continue, tick tick tick tick. Dr Finn noticed my eyes stalking the clock above him as his words failed to jump the 10 foot gap between our seats. He stopped his sentence and joined my curious encounter with the clock, he would look at the clock then back at me, then repeat the process for a few cycles. Second after second the cylinder continued to sing its monotone hymn to the room, to me. The bookshelf near the far right behind his cushioned seat peaked over Dr Finn's round head as the words pinned to the spines of the covers stated their bold font names. The paintings made by past children were scattered along the white walls to give them color perhaps or maybe to distract others from the reason they were here. The reason I was here.

Dr Finn allowed me to observe the clock a few more loud ticks before he made a second attempt to cross the ravine between us. He started off with the simple question of how my day had been. My lips moved as my eyes remained strained on the simple clock, good I said, and yours? He gave a chuckle, whether it was a nervous one or legitimate one I couldn't tell. For I said nothing funny. Had he remembered a joke told to him earlier? His eyes dropped from me to the clock then back as he replied that he had been good as well, he was tired after a long day of paperwork and other tasks. Ticks echoed through the room as no words were spoken for a good amount of small ticks, then Dr Finn began to stir. He sat up and attempted conversation again with some newly found confidence after a signal sip of his coffee, he spoke in a calm manner trying not to startle or spook me like a hunter persuading a deer to lay down and die.

The ticks went on as our conversation continued, my eyes eventually lost interest in the clock but my ears continued to drift off every now and then to the consistency of the beat. 30 Louder ticks past when Dr Finn became tired of my alluding answers, he wanted facts, he wanted my opinion. He asked about my step mom and what I thought of her and my dad's recent marriage, how I felt about it, and how my mother felt about it. Then on the topic of my mother he asked how she was doing financially, if she was able to provide care for me and my brother. Each question more complicated than the last, answers raced in my mind trying to be vague but not too vague where it would lead to another brain throbbing question, until finally I had had enough. Enough of the targeting of my mother, the questions to try and make her seem like a bad parent, the questions that tried to give my dad evidence in the trial that he was the hero in this twisted story.

I was ready to let my rage at him come springing out, to let it devour him in a storm of swears and slurs when all of a sudden something changed. The tone, the pitch, maybe the timing, all I know is that the ticking changed. I calmed myself and listened, I remembered what I was doing here. I wasn't here to give this divorce doctor the evidence he needed, to let him see an ungrateful rude child scream at him, I wasn't here to give him what he wanted, an easy script to write to the court. I was here to stall for time.

NANA BY CASEY WINKLER

There she sits sunk into the tan, cushioned, lounge chair cuddled up with a gray knit blanket. The light peaks through the blinds as the sun warms the small room. Her ipad sits in her lap with a poker app on the screen while she flips through the numerous channels on the television. Typically, she will choose one of the many news channels to watch, but occasionally she'll decide to switch it up and land on a movie or old show. The chair closest to the hallway is where she usually sits, so she can have the shortest walk to the kitchen or bathroom when necessary. Any day of the year she will choose coffee over food which surprises most, but a small cup of decaf coffee can last her hours.

If you know my nana, then you know that there is nothing she loves more than her grandkids. She has the soul of an angel, and a heart of gold. My favorite thing about her is her laugh. As simple as it is, it can take me out of any bad mood. I think everyone deserves to hear this amazing sound at least once in their life. As she laughs I can feel the love and happiness come out into the universe. The smile that comes along with her laugh is one of the most precious things that this world has to offer. She was put on this earth to be a grandmother.

The other week my sister got married, and she and my nana had a promise to each other since she was a little girl that she would sit on her lap on her wedding day. Although she is old and fragile, and another human on her lap might crush her, she stayed true to her word. It was so touching to watch this event happen because I know it was something they both had been looking forward to forever. I will always remember the gestures she did to make her family happy. This is probably my favorite one to date, but others include showing up to all of our sporting and dance events, and cooking with her children on holidays. Her love for holidays is another thing I will carry on and remember. Our holidays are built around her. She makes the world's best dishes such as chicken and dumplings and her famous kolaczki cookies.

Her house during Christmas turns into a winter wonderland. She spends weeks decorating her house with everything imaginable, and will even come to my house to help us decorate as well.

My favorite days that I spent with her was when I was younger. My cousin and I used to have sleepovers at her house, and everything felt so calm. We'd watch a movie or play some games, and she always made us the best popcorn in the world. The aroma from the late night snack lingers through the house throughout the next couple of days. Butter and salt would fill the air and the scent was stronger than any candle I've ever smelt. For some reason, we would also always ended up eating pb&j sandwiches. Probably because that's what was easiest, but every time I take a bite into this incredible sandwich I'm brought back to the days my cousin and I would jump on her bed until she finally convinced us to go to sleep.

I think my nana deserves to know that she is like no other. Her love has had the biggest impact on everyone in my family, and I want her to know that everything we have is because of her. On Saturday night I went over to her house, and she told me how proud she was of her grandkids, and my response was "You're the reason we are who we are. You created this family". And it's true. She is the reason I am who I am today. She has shown me the meaning of love and I love harder every day because so does she. I think every kid growing up looks up to their grandma, and don't get me wrong I still do, but now I can confidently say that I have turned into a mini her and will carry on her ways long after she's gone.

STORYTELLER : CHRONICLE OF A READER TURNED WRITER
BY SANA MUNEER

I spent my childhood weekends in the most magical place on Earth. However, it wasn't filled with roller coasters or arrays of costumed characters. Smelling of ink and fresh paper, my favorite place in the world was home to elderly, sweater-wearing ladies and towering shelves filled with every type of adventure imaginable. Hefting a book-filled bag covered in colorful pins and patches, I skipped through double doors into my version of Disney World: the Glen Ellyn Public Library.

I've been a reader for as long as I can remember; it's the title that best defines me. My childhood was composed of pirate encounters, sword fights, and journeys through the depths of the jungle, all experienced from a familiar blue couch within the library. The adrenaline of finding a new story from my favorite fantasy shelf was a thrill that sparked goosebumps up my arms.

I became utterly immersed in the wondrous world of literature, so much so that my parents found themselves threatening to hide my treasured books if I did not take out the trash or complete my math homework.

After years of devotion to the same library shelves of fantasy and realistic fiction, I realized I wanted more out of the literature I was consuming. I was enthralled by worlds that my favorite authors created, and was eager to develop my own. In fifth grade, I began to pen my own whimsical stories, venturing from my comfy blue chair in the library's Kidz Zone to the activity table lined with blank journals and markers. It was liberating to create a brown-skinned heroine who resembled me. Scribbled in a purple marker were the chronicles of this talkative, free-spirited girl who struggled with math and loved her cat. Everything I had yearned to see in books, like my skin tone, race, and gender, was present in my creations.

As I matured and realized my world was more complex than it had seemed, my frequent visits to the fantasy shelves evolved into exploring the nonfiction section of the library; politics and social justice had become my new stories of choice. I resisted inheriting my parents' belief system and cultivated my own opinions through research on the clunky library computers and hours spent on my blue couch reading Michelle Obama's memoir. Instead of simply reading about the history of the past, I read about the history I was living through and sought out new adventures to find more.

It was in 2018 on a chilly Saturday morning, and the chants from a "March for our Lives" protest echoed throughout the streets next to the library. While taking a stand against gun violence, I was interviewed by a Chicago newspaper. Shifting under the watchful eye of a recording camera, I felt the weight of my voice as I spoke, fully opening up with my bold opinions. I felt newly empowered by this simple act of speaking without inhibition. It was my first encounter with a reporter, and I felt the familiar goosebumps I had while reading a novel rise on my skin while I spoke to her. I understood the importance of having an active voice and knew I had found my calling.

The immersive stories I devoted my childhood to not only solidified my identity as a reader but propelled me into writing. As I glean new journalistic knowledge with every school newspaper article published and broadcast produced for the school announcements, I embrace my new identity as a storyteller, ready to make her own voice heard.

Every time I venture back to the Glen Ellyn Public Library, whether it's to pick out a new book or construct my next news article, I remember my eleven-year-old self devoted to fabricating stories, eager to share them with the world.

WHAT'S THAT?
BY MATTHEW ATLAS

"What's that?" she asked me. My mind is racing, it's stupid, I think. Just carrying around this small thing. I notice my grip clutching it tighter. Do I tell the whole story? Do I just pretend not to hear? What should I say? "Nothing" I replied and put it back in my pocket. I was expecting more questions throughout the day, but none came until the last period of the day. Of course the question was "What's that?" I go through the same process in my brain as earlier. This time I respond with "Long story" and then I proceed to get back to work.

At home I was debating if I should bring it again. It's really helped my anxiety - that voice in my head making my life a living hell, since it makes me feel closer to my grandma whenever I have the stupid thing with me. I decided to bring it again. Nobody really asked about it yesterday so I'm not expecting many questions today. People probably don't even care. I'm just one kid out of the hundreds that go here. It's nothing special, just something my grandma got me for Christmas, the big holiday we celebrate. Her last one. In the middle of the day I'm asked yet again, "What's that?" I go to put it back in my pocket but she grabs my hand and I don't know what to do. I just say "It's stupid" but she won't take that for an answer. She says "I don't care, I'm your friend. Tell me what it is." If I tell her, I know I'm going to be ranting within the next minute, but I decided that I should tell her.

"It's what my grandma got me for Christmas this year." I say. "It makes me feel close to her when I'm in school." I look up and see that in her face she knows why I didn't want to say that. She knows my grandma has stage 4 cancer. She knows that my grandma is dying. "That's not stupid" she said. "Why would that be stupid?" she asked. "I don't know" I say, "Maybe because it's a fricken Catwoman stuffed toy and I'm 16 and carrying it around like a baby." I responded sarcastically. She looks at me with a smile on her face. "What?" I snapped. I didn't mean for it to come out that way. I knew it would happen though. She shouldn't have pushed me. "That's one of the sweetest things I've ever heard," she responded. "Even if you do look like your four years old carrying that around" she finished jokingly. "Shut up" I quip. A genuine smile creeping onto my face for the first time in a few weeks.

A MAPLE FRAMED MEMORY
BY REGANNE NASH

Glancing out of the raindrop-painted window, I watched as a squirrel hops around a pile of amber leaves searching for acorns. Above him the sky is stained a dusty blue- gray hue. He continued his quest until a sudden blaring whistle blew, causing him to scurry away into a nearby bush.

The 5 pm Chicago metra shook the library floor as it passed and I was pulled back from my mid-study window break. As I reviewed my notes, I couldn't contain myself from glimpsing back through the maple framed window that displayed, in my opinion, a piece of artwork more valuable than a Van Gogh oil on canvas: the season of autumn.

Autumn has always been my favorite season. Some may say this is because of my birthday being smack in the middle of the season. However, what truly intrigues me about the season is how, despite the fact that everything is seemingly "dying," the outdoors is more lively than any other time of year.

There's a sense of urgency during the season of autumn, not enough to worry someone, but just enough to spark motivation in an individual. People and animals alike begin to realize the scarcity of the gratifying weather, and attempt to use the last bits of warmth before winter arrives. From ensuring there are enough acorns, to taking a bike ride with friends before the roads turn to ice, every creature is out enjoying the season.

MARLENE   BY SANA MUNEER

Marlene is the newest member of my family.

At first glance, the name 'Marlene' might lead one to assume I got a pandemic pet. However, Marlene is not a cat or a dog. She's a car, a used 2004 Acura that belonged to my grandfather.

My grandfather passed away from congestive heart failure just days after I turned sixteen. His health had been declining for a few months, but between my Mom shielding me from the worrisome details and Covid-19 social distancing, I was largely unaware of how serious his condition had become. This loss was a stark contrast to his everyday presence in my life. My retired grandfather had dutifully picked up my brother and I from school every day since I was in kindergarten. He took great pride in this job, believing it to be the most important task in his day. After secret trips to Dunkin Donuts for a sugary after-school snack, we would go to the library so I could exchange my completed stack of books for a collection of new ones.

Chatting about my busy school day, the magical books I was reading, and my limitless future, I would confide in him how I did not envision myself following in the footsteps of the many doctors in my family. He listened attentively, encouraging me to pursue my unique, creative dreams. I knew from an early age that medicine was not my destiny; my right brain differed from their scientific minds. As we drove through the streets of my town, my grandfather made certain I knew I could choose my own path.

As the pandemic and remote teaching endured, my grandfather missed picking us up from school and spending time in our home, a void we all felt. However, when it came time for us to finally return to in-person learning, he was no longer fit to drive. His car now sat untouched in his garage, free of donut crumbs and library books.

Eventually, we brought his car to my home so I could practice my driving skills. It felt surreal to be in the driver's seat, a throne I had only seen my grandfather occupy.

My birthday weekend in May I had long planned to get my driver's license was one I had been anticipating for months. However, that weekend was instead spent mourning his tragic passing.

His car was no longer a prized possession, but a stinging reminder of his absence and my now bittersweet childhood memories with him. It sat neglected in my driveway, as I grew resentful of its unwelcomed entrance into my life.

Later that summer, when I finally gained the courage to get my driver's license, I decided to rename the car. Referring to it as 'Grandpa's car' stirred up a deep sadness. I named her Marlene Mohsin, a nod to my grandpa's name and my favorite small but mighty character in my most cherished books, the beloved Harry Potter series.

When I drive Marlene through the same streets my grandfather once chauffeured me through, I fondly recall his inspiring guidance and messages of encouragement. Now that I am in the driver's seat, I feel empowered to follow my unconventional dreams with complete freedom. Courage surges through me when I turn the key in the ignition and embark on a new, uncharted goal. I feel like the freest person alive as I navigate my journalistic passions and community-building endeavors. As I look in the rearview mirror at my family's scientific accomplishments, I no longer feel tethered to those expectations. Windows down, I feel a gust of self-driven motivation to tackle challenging social injustices and exercise my voice for the marginalized and most vulnerable members of our community.

Marlene no longer represents the sorrow she once did. Rather, she symbolizes the license I have to defy stereotypes and pave my own unique, unwritten story.

DERSAADEET (DOOR TO HAPPINESS)
BY MISHAL ALLAHRAKHA

The smell of roasted nuts carries down the street as I hear a language foreign to me yet somehow comforting, falling on the tip of every passerby's tongue. Friendly smiles are passed around as the sound of the nearby ocean fills the air. Tourists rush in and out of the never ending bazaar which is surrounded by such an aroma of sweets and spices that are held within. I grip tightly on the bag as I walk in the direction of my hotel, unable to contain the joy within me. Although I am a little bit lost, the contagious energy fills me with a certainty that I will get to where I need to be, if I just keep my feet moving.

As I walk up the alley made of cobblestone which seems to have been there for too many years, a small mewl echoes around me. I turn to see a little ginger kitten making its way to me. I smile to myself and pull out a small bottle. Finally, the moment I have been waiting for. I pour out a few sips worth of the stark white milk that were left in the bottle into the clear bottle cap. The tiny cat immediately circles around me in uncontainable excitement. As soon as the milk is placed on the floor, the cat jumps to it. I smile once more at the tiny thing, and turn to throw the worn plastic bottle in a nearby bin. Rays of light warm my back, signaling the prime of the day. A breeze rushes past the chiffon of my dress as I turn toward the hotel. I have reached my destination. A tall building stands high like the others in the surrounding area with sounds of chatter coming from open windows in all directions. Freshly laundered clothes move with the wind on the thin line they are hung on. Small children run past the flowers and to the corner store for some freshly baked sweets. I close my eyes in contentment as the aroma of the Turkish tea brewing from within the homes reaches my nose. I take a deep breath to imprint the smell within me.

Kathy Georgieva / Untitled

Suddenly, my eyes snap open in surprise. A tall man rushes from within the hotel and motions for me to let him hold the large bag on my arm. With no hesitation, I give a thankful smile and hand it over as I whisper a thank you. The old man opens his mouth to respond but shuts it again. A slight confusion is held in his eyes. My eyes widen at the realization. "Teşekkür ederim."(Thank you.) The words fumble out of my mouth in a strange accent that must have been senseless to him. The stranger smiles brightly at me. His eyes shining with pride of his culture and home. Once again the man opens his mouth and lets out a raspy, "hoşgeldin genç!"(You're welcome, young one!) Strange, isn't it? A mere 12 hour flight from my home, yet the comfort that surrounds me is unmatched. Who would have thought I would be here? A new place is checked off my bucket list, a place that seemed like it would stay on the list for years. Yet I couldn't think of any place greater to be.

Descriptive Sketch.

POST-APOCALYPSE

STEEL

BY SAFA KAMAL

The entire world was in ruins.

Flames danced cheerfully in large splutters with no end in sight. The hues mixed and fought one another in an eternal battle. They snarled and nipped at anything that came close, unsparing of a single soul.
Clouds of heavy smoke lingered above, as they had for quite some time now. They showed no signs of dissipating, and the ominous gray blocked the sun's beams so that the landscape could only enjoy the barest hints of sunlight. Plants had begun withering, the grass and leaves having lost their vibrancy almost completely. Crumbled concrete lay haphazardly, and every building had transformed into ruins. Glass shards glittered dangerously where they were scattered, and lamp posts loomed above menacingly, casting shadows which overlapped with one another. A crack that ran deep into the endless abyss of the Earth split the road into two before running through the old park, and had destroyed whatever it could. It had snapped trees in half with brutal force, leaving only the remaining splinters and branches left.

On one of the only remaining park benches, a boy sat, no older than twelve, humming to himself and swinging his legs childishly. His lightly curled hair bounced with every bop of his head, the shade so dark that it matched right in with his surroundings. The oversized hoodie he wore was stained and battered, but clearly well loved. It appeared as if it would have belonged to the boy's father rather than the child himself, but there was no other being in the area.
The humming broke off into a raspy cough, which was unsurprising with all the dust particles floating around like little fairies. After he had finally calmed himself down, his dull blue eyes traced the ground in front of him. The dry soil was crumbling beneath his feet, and he kicked some right into the crack in front of him. The angle he was sitting at was dangerous, and if he leaned forward some more, he would fall right into the pit.

He vacantly contemplated what would happen if he were to just throw himself in.

"We have rights, so who is Carnegie to deny us from what we were born with?"

Murmured voices filled the union's small hall, both grudgingly certain and uncertain as they observed the man standing in front of them wearily. He had arrived a year ago, bright eyed and bushy tailed, unaffected by the cold and dreary environment that surrounded him.

Even as time wore on, his attitude never dissipated into hopelessness, even as he stared at the meager earnings that filled his coin pouch. Instead, he had brought forth ideas of unions, a thing that many of them had filed away as a distant hope that would never come into existence with the overbearing presence of Carnegie's steel grip.

Hundreds of men sat huddled together, the conditions that they worked in reflecting grotesquely on their bodies. Most, if not all of them, had sunken eyes and hollowed cheeks, with their nails stained, but intact if they were lucky. Some were missing fingers or toes, and others were missing teeth, an eye or both. The constant smoke had resulted in a lingering cough for a majority of the men, and their throats were dry and rubbed raw.

The man opened his mouth, and words of suffering spilled out like molten lava, bright and dangerous, but something that glared right at them. His eyebrows were furrowed and the glint in his dark eyes exuded wrath and pain, a feeling which unfurled amongst the people watching him.

A few weeks later, bodies were filled with large holes, and the sheen of determined eyes was wiped away as they stared unseeingly from where their owners lay motionlessly on the ground. The only solace they could find was that their loss and regrets would be one of many that would lead to victory in the future.

However, it wasn't something they would ever know, not with the red slowly staining the dirt and few blades of dulled green grass.

CRUSH IN THE PARK
BY CHRISTIAN CARTER

A man sits on a bench near the water, surrounded by bustling trees, looking over the lake. He's comfortably dressed, sporting a jacket and khaki pants paired with a beanie, sitting atop his jet-black locks. To anyone watching him from afar, he seems assured and confident, but after getting a closer look at him, he doesn't appear to be at ease. Every few seconds, he observes his surroundings, then stares at the ground, taking tiny breaths of air. The man can do nothing but twiddle his thumbs and tap his feet on the concrete.

One, two, three. One, two, three, his heart was beating so intensely, he could feel it emerge from his chest and exit his body. With his nerves taking control, he tried to catch his breath but couldn't. His mind was racing between having no thoughts to overthinking everything about himself. 'Did I dress right? What if I say something wrong? What if she doesn't even like the park?' Sweat dripped down his face to his lap, and when wiping the liquid off, he put his hands in his pockets, and his hood covered his face. Accepting defeat, the man lowered his face and stared at the ground underneath him.

On the other side of the bench, sits a woman. She was the most attractive woman he had ever laid his eyes on, but he couldn't bring himself to look at her, even sitting feet away from him. She was positioned on the opposite end of the bench, close enough for the man to speak with her but far enough so he could gather his thoughts. He wanted to initiate the conversation, but no words escaped his lips until he decided it was best to stay quiet. And so they sat in silence, just four feet away from each other, both afraid of each other.

She turned her face away to gaze upon the water, and he cautiously moved his attention onto her face. She didn't seem nervous. In fact, she didn't have any hesitation at all. No trembles, no stutters, nothing but her enchanting, gorgeous self. The wind carefully blew her hair into place, resting lightly on her back. Bright shades of red were lightly stroked across her cheeks, which elevated her already picturesque smile.

The man couldn't see her eyes, but he could picture them beaming in front of him. They were overfilled with life and prosperity and had a glow that not even the stars could compare to. She was so calm and collected, and the man, a nervous wreck, never imagined they would ever meet and speak again. It was now or never, he had to make his move. He had strength like cattle, defeated his inner demons, and summoned the courage to speak one-on-one with her. He couldn't say much, choking on his own tongue and the man only managed to sloppily get out one word.

"Hi."

Max Domecka / Ripple Into The Past

KORIKO BAY
BY REGANNE NASH

A gentle summer breeze blows from Koriko Bay, reminding the town of Zephyrus' presence. Spread across the sky, lavender-stained clouds float westward in front of an auburn backdrop. The eventide songs of seagulls begin as the sun utters its goodbyes before a night of rest. With elbows indented from the stone wall her arms rest upon, a girl stands looking out above the azure tide below. Hazel-hued eyes encapsulated by the view ahead, the girl doesn't even notice as the terrain across her arms changes from plains to mountains, chilled by the twilight. Behind her, golden strands of hair dance with the breeze, in complete sync with the waves across the coast. Having no particular place to be, she stays unmoved, pondering the new chapter of life that is about to commence. Despite her childhood nearing a conclusion, she is not quite prepared to leave her adolescence, fearing what adulthood has in store. Muffled gray feline paws leap upward beside her, her one companion during an era of transformation. To the left, on the corner of a boulevard stretching backward, an amber-roofed, yellow-painted bakery sits. A waft of freshly baked pastries drifts towards the girl, tempting her senses. Hints of tart blueberries and candied strawberries overtake her brain, overriding any previous worries. In the distance, the chimes of bike bells ring as young children ride into the night. Overhead, a youthful voice greets hello, another individual at the beginning of independence. Lips mimicking the crescent rising as evening nears, the girl exchanges a grin before finally turning towards the bakery.

SANTORINI, GREECE
BY MISHAL ALLAHRAKHA

The salt of the ocean carries in the light breeze. The sound of sandals hitting the pristine stone below ricochet off the houses surrounding. Crystal waters splash against the wide rocks at bay. The heat blazes off the coal black sand. The stark white of the village houses wrap around the island, covered in domes of bright blues. Laughter and wine is passed around the crowd, as pictures of the sunset are snapped. A sense of tranquility fills the air as bright hues of orange and pink wave through the sky. The sun peeks out from the top of the continuous, rippling navy waves. The bricks of lava that make up the Castle of Oia, glistens in the bright tints that color the sky.

Script.

A SHOT IN THE DARK   BY HANS HERRERA

'A Shot in the Dark' Script Premise: *Over the course of five scenes, a young man runs into the same five characters. Through his interactions with them, he comes to understand his place in the universe as he realizes the detrimental effects that his impact has on others. This tragicomedy was written for the Glenbard South Theatre as the performance space and a transient set made of chair, a table and other props.*

General Summary Up to Scene Four:

Scene One -"Who Are You": *A young man with no name undergoes a job interview, however when he can't even answer his Interviewer's most basic questions, he begins to unravel. The two come to realize the difference between his memories and his feelings. Despite John Doe's shortcomings, he somehow manages to receive the job.*

Scene Two -"What Do You Want?": *John Doe sits at a diner where he soon runs into a pair of twins arguing. After they resolve their argument they begin to interrogate the young man. While they bicker, a middle aged woman gets blackout drunk in the corner. The Interviewer enters wearing a balaclava, and begins stalking the patrons as they converse. As the interrogation intensifies and the middle aged woman becomes aggressive, the Interviewer raises a concealed gun and shoots the ceiling.*

Scene Three -"Are You Ok?": *The Characters-Actors convene to celebrate John Doe's birthday at a park, but as they sing, the Interviewer drops dead. The group freaks out at the corpse and becomes caught up in how he will be remembered. They eventually decide to celebrate his life through a bizarre funeral dance. During the revelry, the Relative suddenly has a click-crisis (explained in script), causing her to become catatonic. After the celebration, the group splits up, and John Doe meets the Aid. They banter and discuss metaphysics until the Aid reveals they are in love with the young man. John Doe becomes willing to take a chance with them and they begin to dance together.*

CHARACTER BIOGRAPHIES:

John Doe - Audience-insert. A young amnesiac who is always at some level of afraid or confused, even if he can hide it very well at times. You, me, them, us.

THE CHARACTER-ACTORS:

The Interviewer - *A representation of "Destiny" and "Time" in the form of an under-the-weather office worker, maybe an ophthalmologist. He is not God, but he is still somewhat ethereal. He is a teacher in some way, he asks questions while already knowing answers, not because he needs to know but because you do.*

The Aid - *A representation of "Love" and "the comfort one can get from relationships" in the form of a twenty-something optimist. They look past pain and flaws, guided to hope and compassion that people are capable of enacting unto the world around them.*

The Goal - *A representation of "Want" and "the expression of desire" in the form of a pretentious hipster who appears to be British. Believing words have a larger impact than actions, they wax poetic on everything, debating and swindling with loopholes and half-truths. The twin sibling of the Gambit.*

The Gambit - *A representation of "What One is Willing To Do To Get What They Want" and "acting upon desire" in the form of a vulgar, rugged yet androgynous figure in clashing clothing and a slight Southern twang. Believing actions speak louder than words, they move impulsively, often doing without disclosing and acting out of proportion. They advise others to do the same. The twin sibling of the Goal.*

The Relative - *A representation of "Uncanny Valley" and "Unsolicited Thoughts" in the form of a middle-aged woman. She is the existential crisis, the mental breakdown. She is the police sketch, a distortion of features yet still recognizable. She is the Relative, estranged, worse-off, and distant, but one can still see themselves within her and still somehow in one's life. She brings out the worst, and won't let you forget it.*

A SHOT IN THE DARK - TRANSITION THREE

As expected, stage deconstructs once again. Yet something is off, perhaps it's the bittersweet air, the soft tune of a slow-dance, the wonder of meta-physics, but the performers move calmly. They walk instead of their normal frantic pace, lifting and removing the bench, shifting the table to center stage and laying a black cloth atop. Someone places a cross above it. A grave. A train whistle releases one short blast followed by one long blast. While this all occurs however, the Relative does not move. She can't. She stares and waits, thinking. She is the only one there as…

LIGHTS UP TO:

SCENE FOUR: EXT. CEMETERY—"WHY DID YOU DO IT?"

Dull. Cold. Beautiful grey skies feel tainted in ashen melancholy. Quiet. A gust of wind echoes through the theater. A soft siren follows suit. The tomb is plain. Cloaked and minimal, an obligation to burial rather than a want. The Relative awaits. Blank. Off. An end to life. A descent into hell.

The young man stumbles in, chuckling to himself. He still has a mark of enthusiasm from the previous scene. He sighs before noticing the middle-aged woman kneeling.

JOHN DOE: Oh, I'm sorry I didn't see you there. Hi! I'm…(*trying to think of what to say instead of his name*) me.

He extends his hand. There's no response.

JOHN DOE: You okay? You seem dazed.

THE RELATIVE (*softly*): He's dead.

JOHN DOE (*looking around, remembering where he is*): Ohh, right. Well, I'm sorry for your loss.

THE RELATIVE: He's dead.

JOHN DOE: I-I know. I was there too. I'm guessing he meant a lot to you.

THE RELATIVE: He's dead.

JOHN DOE: Yes. I'm sorry ma'am. It must've been awful for you, you're still so *frazzled*.

He takes a step closer to her. She looks up to him, a stare of disillusioned wonder.

THE RELATIVE: How well did you know him?

JOHN DOE (*slightly surprised at a new answer*): Well, he got me my job, and while I heard he had a couple tricky situations in the diner and whatever, he did show up at my birthday party before ya' know, DYING. (*realizing what he said*) Sorry, that was insensitive. How did you know him?

THE RELATIVE: I-I don't know.

He approaches her further, attempting to put a hand on her shoulder.

JOHN DOE (*slight chuckle*): Huh, I know what that feeling's like. Look I'm really sorry this happened to you. I get that you can't remember all the details—

THE RELATIVE: Don't touch me.

He rescinds his hand, instead choosing to kneel down across from her. She continues to look up, despite his new location.

JOHN DOE: Sorry. But you still have feelings right? You feel that you miss him. You cared for him and thought about him and maybe even loved him. But he's gone.

THE RELATIVE: He's dead.

JOHN DOE (*not taking this seriously*): Ope, here we go again. And I'm sorry for that, very. But—

THE RELATIVE: He had a life. He had me, he had you. For chrissake, he had all of us. But now you're gone.

JOHN DOE: Do you mean he's—

THE RELATIVE: You all left. You didn't care, you didn't know, you didn't want to know. And now he's gone.
The young man is slightly taken aback, not offended but confused.

JOHN DOE: Look lady, I sorry that this happened to you but I think you're letting grief get to you. I'm sure you're feeling that you have to mourn but I don't know if you're all there. Maybe you have to move on.

She lowers her to meet his gaze, still and sternly. A thousand yard glare. He continues to ramble.

JOHN DOE (*cont'd*): I think that maybe you're feeling stuck. That in this vast universe there's no one here. But there are. And people will leave but you can still have memories. You can make new ones too. Ya' know before I was a wreck. Like I couldn't remember anything, like I was weirded out and confused by everything… and it— it sucked. But I found love, I found that happiness and I went from black and blue to… well, better. I went forward and made new thoughts. And I got a special someone now! It's awesome. (*a beat*) Yeah, I know he's dead. I know that I'm not you and I can't think like you. I'm not in your head. I am completely different! On a whole different plane from you! Like I'm loud and you're quiet. I'm happy and you're sad. I'm young and you're— Sorry. I-I should stop now. (*a beat, playfully*) Why are you staring at me like that? Am… is there something on my shirt or something? Stop it. Come on, hey. It's gonna be okay, okay?

The Relative still stares.

THE RELATIVE: Why did you do it?

JOHN DOE: Sorry?

Still kneeling, she raises from slouched and sitting to a tall, beaming form.

THE RELATIVE (looking down at him): Why are you still doing it?

JOHN DOE: Um… I don't really know how to respond to that—

THE RELATIVE: Listen to your own goddamn words, why is this happening?

JOHN DOE: I…do you mean his death? I—I had nothing to do with—

THE RELATIVE (picking up pace): Yes. You. Did. And it's not just that. You're "hopey-popey" treatment. Before. After. Still. You hurt him.

JOHN DOE (stunned): I…what? No, I…I have to go. I wish you well but—
As he gets up to leave, the Relative swiftly grabs hold of his wrist.

THE RELATIVE: Stay.

JOHN DOE (very uncomfortable): No, stop that.

He pulls back. Her grip remains.

THE RELATIVE: No. Right now, you have to stay.

JOHN DOE: No, please, let go. You're hurting me. I have to—

THE RELATIVE (violently): I SAID STAY!

As the young man attempts to retract his arm, the Relative forcefully shifts their weight, throwing her unwilling compatriot across the floor. John Doe lays stunned as the wind is knocked out of him.

JOHN DOE: WHAT THE HELL LADY!

THE RELATIVE: Oh, will you just shut up for once?

JOHN DOE: Well, I want to know why you just threw me to th—

THE RELATIVE: Why did you do it?!? Why, out of everything you could have done, did you do it?

JOHN DOE: I HAVE KNOW IDEA WHAT YOU'RE EVEN TALKING ABOUT!

THE RELATIVE: This! Here! This was not the goddamn plan, because you just had to go, and you *had* to hurt him.

JOHN DOE: I did not hurt him! I don't even know who you're talking about. Cause if this is about my boss's death, I'm sorry but I HAVE NOTHING TO DO WITH IT. Just get that in your head because whatever junk you have going on up there, its—

THE RELATIVE: YOU HURT HIM! Just admit it, that for once on this god-forsaken plane, that someone else is struggling more than you, that your actions are more than just self-righteous internal pity. Because guess what? You're not dignified, you're deluded, a destroyer. Your cutesy little "safe space"? It doesn't exist. Admit it.
A pause, the young man has no idea what to say. Suddenly something clicks: feelings of dread, euphoria, calm, and terror quickly flood through him. An existential epiphany. But as soon as it surged in, it ebbs away. He tries anyway.

JOHN DOE: Look, I—I'm sorry. I didn't want to—I never wanted to hurt him. It wasn't my intention, please, look I—

THE RELATIVE: Oh, but you did, and look where we are now. Stuck. Gone. Everything in your pathetic life led to this. Every mistake, every humiliation, every loss and struggle and stupid decision you've made has brought you HERE!

She holds out her hand, extending all five fingers before pointing at herself.

THE RELATIVE (*losing control*): These are the FRUITS of your labor!

JOHN DOE: Stop it. That's not me. I'm not—

THE RELATIVE (*sickly sharp*): Oh because we get it, you won, and you got the job-

JOHN DOE: I'm more than-

THE RELATIVE: What? More than what? You think you're tough huh, that you can just breeze past death? Well none of us are. I'm tough. I'm more than all of you.

JOHN DOE: What are you—

The Relative proceeds to pull out her lighter and a cigarette. Fumbling, she lights it.

THE RELATIVE: This is tough.

She takes a puff before immediately slamming the red-hot end into her palm, trying to hide her pain.

THE RELATIVE (*through her teeth*): Gah!

JOHN DOE: What were you thinking, you're gonna burn a hole in your hand!

THE RELATIVE: I'm showing you a lesson, of everything you're not.

She thrusts the cigarette at him before throwing it to the ground.

JOHN DOE: By mutilating yourself?!? Look, I have a whole LIFE, it's not just—

THE RELATIVE (*breaking further*): So they loved you, well—well he loved you, but—but now, now he's, he's—

JOHN DOE: I CAN'T BE EXPECTED TO DO EVERYTHING RIGHT—

THE RELATIVE (*shattered*): HE'S GONE!!!!! MY MAN, MY BOY, MY… (*a breath, shifting down to loveless*) whatever. It doesn't matter anymore. He's dead, and we're left with *you*. The boy who danced around a dead body forgetting it was even there. You got a corpse for a birthday present, you put a life on display. We are the disastrous forms you made us to be. Your filth, your failure, taught us to be *this*.

The young man is terrified. Battered and bruised, but he's not willing to stand down yet.

JOHN DOE (*unsure then defiantly*): I—No. No, I'm not a failure. I am not afraid of you. I'm not some defect in your life. I am not going to fade into nothingness while you're treating me like this, not again.

THE RELATIVE (*under her breath*): Whether you believe us or not, it doesn't matter. The future will happen, time passes by while we all succumb together. It's up to you.

JOHN DOE: Ok, but… wait. What does that mean? What do you really want from me?

THE RELATIVE (*sarcastically at first*): What do we want, hmm… What do we want from YOU? WE WANT YOU TO WAKE UP!!!

Suddenly a car horn is heard in the distance. From the back of the theater walks down the twins. They continue to bicker but noticeably lack an accent.

THE GOAL: Look, bread bowls are fine, but doughnut holes, now we're talking. Maybe you can buy me some after you know, we deal with this child.

THE GAMBIT: You really think that fried bits of dough are better than soup in an edible bowl? No. After we fix the kid, we're doing you next.

THE GOAL: Preposterous, we're not—

The pair's spat is abruptly cut short as they notice the young man and the middle-aged wreck. They run over to them, frantic.

THE GOAL (*jaw dropped*): YOU. I knew there was something in the air! It smelled more depressive than usual! What is it that you want from us?!?

JOHN DOE: I… what?

THE GAMBIT: No, seriously, why are you doing this to us?

JOHN DOE: Wait, I—

THE GOAL: We get it, you're out of the water, but there are other fish stuck in this barrel!

JOHN DOE: I— what does that even mean?

THE GAMBIT (*kind of normal*): Yeah, to be fair that wasn't a really good metaphor. (*back to frantic*) But, please stop this! Do something!

In walks the Aid as well, abnormally calm compared to the rest of the motley crew.

THE AID: Hello, I suppose we're all coming together now are we?

JOHN DOE (sort of blushing): Oh, um, hi, but what is happening? Why are you all here?

THE AID: Well, long story short, we're here because you're here. We're kind of stuck.

THE GOAL: Yeah, and it's not going to *end* until you leave.

THE GAMBIT: So do it, leave.

JOHN DOE: I… wait. Wait a minute, whoa, whoa, whoa, whoa, whoa, whoa, whoa. Whoa. WHY AREN'T YOU BRITISH?

A rumble. It alerts the entire group. It occurs again. They look around, trying to figure out where the sound is coming from. When it sounds a third time, they all realize it's coming from the grave. A voice is heard from underneath.

THE INTERVIEWER: May I come out now?

JOHN DOE: What?

THE INTERVIEWER: Is it ok for me to come out?

ALL CHARACTER-ACTORS (*at varied tones*): Yes, you can come out.

After a couple more thumps and thuds, from beneath the tomb rises an long-seen face, the Interviewer. The young man is more flabbergasted than one could ever possibly flabbergast.

THE INTERVIEWER: Is everyone caught up?

THE GOAL: No.

THE GAMBIT: Not really.

THE AID: I think he still needs our help.

THE INTERVIEWER: If it is okay with everyone, is it time for us all to intervene together?

JOHN DOE (*finally speaking up*): WHAT THE HELL IS GOING ON?

THE RELATIVE (*bluntly*): You're dreaming.

DROP TO BLACK

Spoken Word Poetry.

ENNUI AND EDUCATION
BY HANS HERRERA

" *No, I'm not alone with*
Little reason and stupid schemes
All of those other students
Still have got their dreams "

HOTTIES OBNOXIOUSLY CRUNCH OUTFITS
BY HANS HERRERA

" *Emotions fuel*
as the wave surge
breaks capri suns
on bejeweled heels "

About the Authors

The authors, poets, and beautiful souls whose work is bound within these pages range from 14-18 years old, range from freshmen to seniors in high school, range all throughout the gender spectrum. They range from bookish introverts to Lady Gaga level spotlight hogs. They range in the breadth of their dreams and how wide their arms can stretch. They range in how much space they are ready to take up and how loudly they say their own names. The one thing they have in common now, thanks to you, is that they are all finally seen for the brilliance that lies within each and every one of them. Thank you for taking the time to see them.

Made in the USA
Middletown, DE
02 May 2023

29895858R00038